I0763612

MISCHIEF

poetry

MISCHIEF

poetry

Hal Hartley

ELBORO

MISCHIEF

poetry

ISBN: 978-1-7379274-6-4

Published in New York by Elboro Press

Elboro Press books may be purchased in bulk for educational, business or sales promotional use. Please address enquiries to:

office@elboropress.com

First Edition, 2024 – First Printing

Principal Sponsors

Bjorn Andersson, Greg Baprawski, Michael Barnstijn,
Andrew Blossom, Julianne Bond, Jerome Brownstein,
Derek Busby, Kathleen Chopin, Kelly Craig,
Cyril Danilevski, Marcy Donelson, Geralyn Dreyfous,
Douglas Elliott, Beth Estrin, R. Michael Fierro,
Nick Ford, brian d foy, David Gamlin,
Stephen Gates, Jason Gessner, Steve Hamilton,
James Hancock, Kurt Hemr, Amer Hilal, Asuka Honda,
Paul Hrissikopoulos, Jennifer Huber, Gregory Jacobs,
Adam Jeal, Toby Jennings, Nicholas Keuler,
Christopher M. Krobath, Kohei Kuribayashi, Mark Lanwehr,
Timothy Latimer, Richard Linklater, Roderick Macrae,
Leah Mason, Jeremy Matthews, Charlie McIntosh,
Werner Messmer, Jim Mickle, Randall Moore,
C&N Moulton, Aidan O'Bryan, Ivan Orlic,
Jay Phelan, Justin Courtney Pierre, Jeremy Riegel,
Neal Robinson, Jim Rodney, Stella Sakadonikolakis,
Sekka Scher, Benjamin Schnieder, Adam Schoon,
Septimus, Jennifer Sheaffer, Hiromi Shindo,
Kenji Shingai, Syngeon Smythe, Michael Spiller,
Tim Stevens, James Szajda, Diana Takata and Don Thompson,
Jack Teuber, Adam Tolkien, Jordi Torrent,
Alex Vacca, Alex Valero, Takuya Watabe,
Bruce Weiss, Andreas Welk, Victoria Wisdom

CONTENTS

MISCHIEF

IN PRAISE

Oh Large One
surpassing all things little,
take favor on us,
your mid-sized ambivalators,
teach us to know more your largeness
and to take proper advantage
of all things littler,
so we may increase in our mediocrity
and pour everlastingly
from emptiness
into the void.

REAL

The virtual yields
sometimes
to the tangles of personality,
hurt feelings in so many kilobytes
per second,
an anticipation crushed
with a misspelt word,
a misuse of jargon or fumbled acronym,
intel drifting further from meaning
    with each concession
to an emoji.

And then the cool light breath,
a voice in the hall,
as he stumbles on to fall and rise
again
like a man without expectation
but hope
who buries himself in her actual neck
and offers himself
as a real
possibility.

BAD CARPENTRY

Suddenly reminded
of what he's always known:
all he has is all he needs.
Though he has more than required he cares
about quality.
An unlevel shelf injures him,
badly made chairs hurt
his ability to be kind,
the evidence of uncaring
labor
or
honest ineptitude
reminding him
he's a snob and,
though he can endure feeling superior,
he's incapable, peaceably,
of existing
with bad carpentry.

DRIFT

The taxi uptown drifts
sideways towards the river on his left,
the tumbling down the embankment
a pleasant respite
from the details of tomorrow's hassles,
the splash unheard
and soft,
unhurtful,
a flattened paper bag of escaping doubt.

Punched by a warm round wind,
he's coughed out the window
and drifts still further
over water
towards Jersey
and up higher too
to where the night is kept
permanently
on view
for those attuned
to the distanced, cadenced, remote
blues
crooned once long ago
and now suspended
infinitely
as he remembers
all the words at last.

She needs he knows
to hear and keep
in her closely guarded phone

his wistful musing and puzzled verse
summoning up and making real
their improbable, unspoken, and chaste intimacy
which, in the telling, may be all there is
but is, at least,
all the words at last.

He drifts back to the west side highway
as the bridge comes into view,
to the taxi again and northward, sleepily
approaching the prison he's earned himself,
where to collect and arrange
the words she needs
to hear and keep
remains his welcoming
lifelong
sentence.

DOGGEREL

Cups of coffee and bottles
of beer,
that's the way he measures distance
up here,
far from his mistress
way downtown,
he takes care of business and tries
not to drown
in the so-much-to-do of it all.
But what, he wonders, is he trying to prove
with all these bills paid promptly
and the torturously composed correspondence
too?
When it's all forgotten,
dispatched, and done
he'll be with her, briefly,
having sexual fun.

APPARENT MOTION

Practically useless to sit
doing little
in the time where nothing can be done
waiting
between pictures.

Watching could be doing for a man who makes
pictures,
though mainly organizing life and business to make
pictures
when he's gifted with the time and resources to make
pictures.

Words are pictures too,
he thinks, or could be
maybe. Why not
make order
from these ecstasies grazed in passing,
the unlistening miseries of the eternal now?

Time is the cross
he bears, he recites,
setting down the present,
hoping to mark the time and,
so marked, threaten all this merely
apparent motion.

DWARVES

Reliable dwarves,
adorable and sane,
their lullaby hymn melting
black ice off the tree limbs and curbs
as they head for the river
and New Jersey
beyond.

Curiosity moves them
philosophy too,
singing across the ice-cluttered Hudson
to their exiled comrades
and New Jersey
beyond.

BRING IT ON

This conscience of mine
as a roof built above
an idea of myself
I pay for,

the obligation to cease to dream
and face
incomprehension,
this punch to the gut, and not
complain.

Why have I provoked
this outrageous lack
of interest?
I could have been elsewhere,
unnoticed and unconcerned.

The evidence is there
for anyone to see,
this world demands much less
than a conscience
of me.

But will I congratulate myself
   for following a path
I cannot avoid
choosing,
or give quarter
to efforts only half made
and countenance cheap fixes yielding
fortuitous shades of, say, subtext

to remain uncorrected and praised
as the intended though casual stroke
of an applied genius?

One must live with oneself I see
and this house now is too old
and ill-equipped
to withstand the damp chill
of flattery.

So bring it on.
For what does not kill me will
kill me
eventually.

And there's time enough for everything.

TO LIVE THERE SIMPLY

To live there simply
without excuse,
the short day's lengthening
solitude
an active quiet,
a fresh amazement,
at twelve
or forty,
some pale low light and the attendant
breath-depleting need
collapsing
beyond bare trees to what must be
the west.

CURMUDGEON

Motor skills loosening
and objects drop
like somebody else's fault.

A cursive essay renders modern art
or an unhelpful map.

Thirty pounds overweight
according to
confidently unsubstantiated websites
marketing unpronounceable medications
targeting the elderly—

Where was I?

A man alone,
no loving, paid help,
useless obligations,
the sad loss of friends to eternity,
resentment,
conspiracy theories,
or the most attractive victimization
lifestyle.

Troubled memories,
vague regrets,
dread of the insane,
and bills to pay.

AMOUR PROPRE

Long after the festival soiree,
flirting outrageously and falling
laughingly through the blurred mitts
of drunken young men,
this wanton groupie at last dances barefoot
on the boutique pension's lobby bar.

Finally she insists that he, the elder statesman,
escort her gallantly
upstairs to her chamber's door,
one of three on the quaint establishment's second
floor,
and quite possibly beside that of a stern,
graceful and revered Persian beauty whose attention
he covets but who that very day questioned,
in public,
the worrisome moral drift
of his latest work.

Still, carrying upstairs this pint-sized waif
whose voice he can hardly bear,
while all he wants, vainly, it's true,
is to refute the lovely Persian's mistaken view,
he knows his bruised feelings are his own affair.

But now his charge at the required door
falls to her knees, leans forward, and searches
her artfully dropped purse for the rumored keys,
her skirt riding up to reveal underwear worth noting
while begging too loudly: Spank me, please!

Jealous of his reputation
and his proudly veiled critic's good regard,
with the promiscuous urchin over his shoulder,
he continues upstairs to his own room
where they stumble from their clothes,
grope, kiss clumsily, but do not go far,
though he obliges finally and spanks her once,
hard.

Eyes wide, sparkling like a Christmas tree on fire,
she descends silently and passes out,
shoulders and cheek to the mattress pinned,
her bare bottom raised in thoughtless defiance,
arrived, finally, unconscious and spent.

Welcoming this brief reprieve and admiring her
unclouded conscience,
he damns himself for his over-sensitivity
to criticism.

Waking to daylight he finds her mistaking
an armoire for a toilette before blindly climbing
onto the window and peeing
sloppily
out onto the rooftop three stories above
the ancient and narrow street.

Don't jump, he begs, guiding her back and
That's funny, she giggles, her bladder relieved,
diving back to the rumpled sheets to sleep
perchance to dream as he packs his bag
and flees.

FOR NOW

Fingers entwined,
palm to palm,
deep in the pocket of his coat.

Is it he who
gently presses
or she in response

to this new confusion,
this timid attraction
shoulder to shoulder,

their conspiracy silencing the preoccupied city
like brave children
with holy secrets and smiles.

ADVENTURES IN READING

I do not study,
the striking, dark-eyed sister
surmised,
to write much less
to teach but only to see
if I, by studying, will be
less ignorant.

The nun in Mexico City centuries ago
wakes him and he, falling
again to her eloquence learns
the Greek *rhapsode* was a bard
not a poet,
a singer covering standards and
is this not the origin of our modern *rapper*?

For instance?

Later, still not dressed for work,
he discovers *murmuration* is really a word,
not just an inspired figuration of the poet-ambassador
who translates the nun and,
while showering,
considers accomplishment and its rewards,
alternately construed
and dismissed
as privilege or entitlement,
no more than work well done
with the means at hand
by whomever has the guts.

What we think as we feel
what we feel,
the ambassador adds, sending our man back
   to the shelves
to consult the Sphinx
at Rio,
a Ukrainian Jewish Latina who doubts she can live
   a Christian hope,
pushing reality to the unreachable future instead
   of an available now.

Vague thoughts, quick impressions,
paralyzing intuition
threatening
to postpone the day
entirely, he ventures
to read endlessly and annihilate
the practical.

Until, his eye falling randomly to the page,
the Sphinx suggests not everything needs to be known
and not knowing is important
too.

Owning his delinquency,
at the mercy of a mental and spiritual thirst
actively distrusted by technological culture,
he unplugs the phone and goes offline,
consulting the English
Woman
he hasn't read since college
but gets lost amongst the volumes and, instead,
finds the socially impossible French

Girl
questioning
the value of her society
and the meaning of her life
while a mid-century American literary critic broods
  hilariously about a rabbi
from twenty-two hundred years ago cautioning:
Avoid the loud of mouth!
Do not heap wood on their fire!

Paralyzed by ideas,
staring down for an hour at the chaos
of a city still managing
to function,
his day's path obliterated,
he wonders who out there has the will to doubt
their particular fire is essential?

He has a beer and submits to the setting sun,
listening still for the mystic mom of Rio
and the seventeenth century nun,
these two long-unknown distant loves,
foreign voices buffeting his dizzy intellect,
igniting his heart with their minds as learning,
the ambassador wrote,
is an audacity, a kind of violence.

Unwilling to retreat from a past he regrets
having not experienced in this company,
insisting there is no time
without boundaries,
the contours of his thoughts and feelings,
as theirs,

phosphorescent amid the day's clamoring data,
he is epileptic
with conscience, speculation,
erotic potential and traffic-stopping lucidity.

But to silence he concedes at last,
falling again,
his mind dulled joyously
to the pillow,
sleeping his way toward the real
unbodied persistence
of the actual.

EVOLVE

Always hoping
to be
perfect
in that moment
events set
aside

for us to be
always
the newest and best
florescence.

We wither
gracefully
instead,
or not, while

others emerge
innocently
ferocious
and hungrier
to expand and glow
as we fade.

ABOUT THIS

Words fail and he hopes
anything possible of saying can be
and help.

Movement, likewise, disappoints
as he falls
back
out of the light and, shy,
afraid of breaking something,
breaks.

A past love passes
away, murdered,
and in the sudden suffocating absence,
an unanswerable violent unmeaning,
a jagged tearing collision with what is
and cannot be undone,
he, so good with words, can only draw
his soul tenderly across fissures
endured and nearly forgotten,
bliss and dumb laughter fondly remembered,
highlighted and felt in a later life
of other loves.

Where, blinded by incomprehension, to turn
while a fierce palsied grief creates a family
of strangers far and wide
howling,
scratched raw by the horror
of a woman's desecrated body,
her extinguished life?

Where to go to hear
his own irregular heart
beat
but to stand in the rain
of this foreign city
remembering
her at twenty-three
jumping up and down on his bed,
naked,
bruising his rib with her heel
as he rolls into her laughing path
—an ache he endures gratefully
and embraces still now
in defiance of animal brutality
an ocean away.

She's the only one
still
he talks to
about this.

LULL

The lull,
the stillness,
a life lying unwatched
upon the surface
of the flood.

Dry quiet hours
free of ambition,
unseen amongst the jostling aspirants,
the flotsam and jetsam
of dubious accomplishment
receding.

INFLUENCER

The oracle lay back, sated,
after another self-inflicted erotic experience
and checked her socials.

Four hundred and twenty-two new friends
in less than an hour.
A mob of emojis: submissive, contrite, or merely
desperate,
her oppressed and victimized followers,
the proudly dismissed and notoriously unneeded,
resentful and happy to be a nuisance
for whomever she requires,
increasing their credit card debt consuming breathlessly
whatever she herself admires.

To fan the flames or just confuse?
She has options, being an avatar.
Sounding White but feeling Black
with an Asian kick-boxing vibe too,
gender-fluid and polyamorous
without a politics other than the need
to succeed.

She consults a list of popular discontents,
weighing the likely news cycle heft of some new
   unfounded provocation
aimed at the conspicuously entitled
and what their outrage might reasonably afford her:
the arrogance of learning,
the violence of knowing,

the tyranny of understanding,
the viscous complacency of charitable endeavor—

She can make this work if she types
LOUD enough.
But a pop song in her earbuds
dispassionately annunciating
a cooler indifference
inspires subtlety.
How, now, to increase hits and tantalize the base
  while demonstrating a plausible conversance
  with forward-looking dialogue and reasoned argument
  to enact practical change without, of course, sounding
  like an accommodation to the fascist liberal educated
  elite who do *not* follow her on Twitter?!!!

Drawing down her panties again
for the paying subscribers,
watching her bitcoin balance increase in real time,
she fingers herself and wonders
what the *hoi polloi* can possibly want
that it cannot accomplish
with a well-conceived, gracefully executed, and sloppy
blowjob?

Figuratively speaking. Or not.

BRUNCH

The emptiness of so much chat,
panicked lapses of joyous comradery
filled with desperate
relief,
gratitude for the most profound
banality.

Impressive, still,
this effort made
to keep spirits up or, at least,
idle and insincere curiosity
plausible.

AUSLÄNDER

Black crows cover the bare limbs
   of the tree in the *hinterhof*
and sleep
as he cannot,
marveling at the dark
light of dawn begging admittance
to the day.

He speaks to them in a German
only they can endure,
their concerns being elsewhere and, after all,
they're Polish crows anyway.
They can afford to indulge him,
watching without expression
as he drifts through these rooms,
his quiet, secluded haven of chosen exile,
bewildering even his Berlin friends who,
like the crows, keep a polite distance
and, to themselves, their thoughts.

Difficult, unreasonable, and contrary—
he's heard what people say.
Or is he merely unstuck from trends,
self-indulgent and passé?
No, he suggests, to the crows, the clear cold Baltic air,
only at the mercy of a taste and sensibility
the excellence of which he does not dare
deny
until proven guilty.
Though perhaps he is washed-up,
out of step

with the times,
misguided,
too shy.

Stepping out into the chill
balcony above the street, he sees
a wild fox trot—
lost, delinquent, fugitive—
up the far sidewalk.

Has he, in fact, chosen loneliness,
lost a wealth of intimacies,
skirted some glossier success by too stringent
an insistence
on principle,
avoiding tempests of emotion to pursue
a loving and unprejudiced
equanimity?

Can he live with himself
by himself
in a language not his own,
with the failures, memories, and conceits,
this gigantic love
he only ever apologizes for,
and bear the weight
of the coming day
again?

LITTLE VICTORIES

Alone and unfocused
on a sidewalk uptown,
the first waves of autumn
chill
remind him to drag
from the dim clutter of basement storage
the winter coat.

Will he resemble the man
of the summer to her
who is always
like spring?

He buys a six-dollar shirt at the discount store
and feels like forty-five bucks,
more or less,
and gets a smile from a passing un-wed mom
with a tattoo.

But will he resemble the man
of the summer to her
who is always
like spring?

IMPROMPTU

He was lucky to get in
early,
later
it was packed.

But before,
beyond
the far corner of the room was the North Sea
or Spain in winter
behind tall plate-glass doors
on wrecked hinges,
the wind off the water driving raindrops mad
against flapping plastic.

The beer tasted like gravel floating
in cigarette smoke.
But the girls were immediately better
looking
as the show business made itself
apparent
in the way young men leaned
closer,
sincerely, even
interested,
with impatience
and fiercely held
plans.

He committed himself
to poetry
as a method of accommodating
the effervescence.

SOME SMALL WAY

Just this
history of mistakes
mitigated
by success
in planning
under pressure,
a salvageable waste
floating
towards a peaceful endurance
of a life
useful
in some small way.

HE’S NOT READY

Awake again with the rhythm of the old,
more than rested but defiant
he pretends not to notice and wrestles back
his attention from the coming day’s toil
to the warm, confused, and evasive notion
of a dream that won’t stand still.

Though not ready, he does sit up
admitting defeat,
appreciating the rattle and clack
of trucks unloading produce
down in the street
and confronts the pre-dawn chill.

No, he’s not yet ready for the daily grind,
the responsibilities he’s made
himself
capable of and willing to address
when fired by ambition,
in broad daylight, to outrage
all offending meaninglessness.

Still, not ready, though resigned,
he admits, “to the barricades!”
and brushes his teeth.

In his chair by the window reading deep
into the past as the coffee brews
he seeks advice,
improving examples,
disquieting clues

in the lives of people
gone before
who completed their allotted span,
sometimes more,
as a name affixed to an acknowledged feat
or, more commonly,
the front of an office building.

What to leave behind, he wonders,
except words, a picture perhaps
a tune or two?

But he's not yet ready, he knows that now.
The sun's already up and today
as yesterday
and all his imagined tomorrows
are mysteries woven
out of stories hammered
into questions asking
How.

NEXT

What to risk suggesting next
without losing
this different excellence,

an attention to moments of grace,
full, yet without
obvious meaning,

the desire to see
free of the habit of seeing with eyes
industrialized,

no longer in the effort to facilitate
the anticipated push and shove
of the recognizable

impoverished
into brave statements of purpose
unbelieved?

What to risk suggesting next
without fantasy or unearned hope
in reading the concrete passage of life's fluid text?

Contributing Sponsors

Kurt Aerden, Philip Aromando, Mary Bernard,
David Bodamer, Michel Bodmer, Andy Bullock,
Michael Cahill, Mark Clark, Greg Cobb,
Cary Cody, Simón de Santiago, Adam Donnelly,
Sarah Eaton, Sally El Hosaini, Francis Glennon,
Christopher Gorman, Thomas Gutmann,
Jack Hartley, Miho Hartley, Nicholas Helfrich,
Erwin Hoorebeke, Don Hunt, Spencer Hunt,
Virany Kreng, Adam Kuntavanish, Franklin Laviola,
Vincent Lefieux, Brian Marino, Menno Metselaar,
Angela Miskis, Christian Monggaard, Jesse Lawrence Morgan,
Vikram Murthi, Karen Nakamura, Christopher Nicotera,
Graeme Pearson, Richard Per, Mark Pescatrice,
Kevin Pitcock, Charles P. Rhoads, John Price Richey,
Haco Saito, Step Schwarz, Yoshinori Sekiguchi,
Dave Simonds, Jennifer Sparks, Jim Sparks,
Rick Spears, Hisashi Takamatsu, Mikihiko Tanaka,
Illona Tobin, Franck Voisin, Rick Webb,
Lawrence Weis, Kira Wizner, Akiko Yamaguchi,
Satoko Yasuda, 姜青俊, さかしたりえ

www.ingramcontent.com/pod-product-compliance
Lightning Source LLC
Chambersburg PA
CBHW060538310726
48982CB00009B/1294/J

9781737927464